This book belongs to:

_____

_____

Contents

First published 2008 by Brown Watson
The Old Mill, 76 Fleckney Road,
Kibworth Beauchamp, Leic LE8 0HG

ISBN: 978 0 7097 1803 1

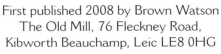

EARLY READERS

Three Read Together Stories

Stories by Gill Davies

Illustrations by:
Gill Guile, Stephen Holmes,
Jane Swift and Lawrie Taylor

Brown Watson
ENGLAND

ARE CHILDREN REAL?

"Are there really any children at the bottom of our garden?" Fairy Rose asks her big sister one day.

"Only now and then," says her sister. "And only really good, kind children can see us, if they open their eyes really wide and are as quiet as mice."

So one day Rose goes to see if she can find one.

Suddenly the grass moves and Rose sees a big face looking down. It is a boy, wearing heavy boots. The enormous boy looks at Rose. He looks really hard – but he cannot see her at all.

Rose stays very still until the boy runs away.

"Now I know it is just a silly story," he yells to his sister. "There are no fairies there."

The next day Rose goes to the end of the garden again and sees another big face looking down at her. This time it is a girl – a good, kind girl.

"Hello," says the girl. "So you are real after all."

"Yes, and so are you," laughs Rose. They both smile, feeling shy but so happy to have found each other at last.

KEY WORDS

any	her
as	if
at	know
big	next
both	only
boy	our
day	so
goes	their

WHAT CAN YOU SEE HERE?

fairies

garden

nose

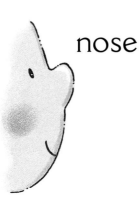

girl

boots

DONKEY DISHES

Donkey is having a tidy up in the barn. Under the hay he finds an old lumpy, bumpy bag.

"Tip it out," says Molly the dog. "Let's see what is inside this lumpy bumpy bag."

Donkey tips the bag up. Out fall lots of bowls.

There are red, blue and white bowls . . . and yellow, pink and green bowls.

"Heehaw! What a lot of bowls," says Donkey. He starts to sing:

"Red and blue, Heehaw! Heehaw! Pink and green . . . two more make four. Yellow and white . . . here are some more."

"Well, what can we do with them all?" asks Molly the dog.

"Fill them," says Donkey. "And then ask all our friends to tea."

So that is what they do.

They fill all the bowls with good food.

They fill the red bowl and the blue bowl and the white bowl . . . and the yellow, pink and green bowls.

Then Horse and Billy Goat and Silly Goat and Cat and Puppy and Hen all come to tea.

KEY WORDS

and	of
bag	out
blue	pink
fall	red
farm	tea
friend	up
green	white
makes	yellow

WHAT CAN YOU SEE HERE?

red barrel

blue bowls

donkey

pink bowls

yellow name tag

SUMMER HAS GONE

Tom is an old train. He is very, very old and slow but he is always happy.

Sam is a new train. He is very new and fast but he is not always happy. Sometimes he feels sad.

"Cheer up," says Tom when they meet. "It is a nice sunny day and the sky is blue."

"But summer has gone," says Sam. "I don't want it to be cold. I want summer to last." He stops: "Oh dear, and now I can't push all these leaves out of the way."

But then a sudden wind sends all the leaves flying off.

"See," says Tom. "Things do work out in the end."

Off go the two trains. Both are smiling.

"Sam is happy at last," says Tom to the cow. "But the leaves have fallen in front of me now. Never mind. I shall blow a big puff of steam and send them flying again. Whoo! Whoo!"

The leaves fly into the sky. Tom rolls on, as happy as can be.

27

KEY WORDS

can't	off
cow	push
do	sky
don't	slow
fast	stops
gone	sunny
I	these
last	train

WHAT CAN YOU SEE HERE?

new train

leaves

passengers

old train

driver